TATE MCGHEE

This Moment in Time

Dedicated to the life and memory of Lisa Sheridan.

Contents

1

Invitation Echoes: A Stir of Emotions

In the spring of 2021, Tom Matthews sat at his cluttered desk, surrounded by theater scripts and old photographs. The crisp, Pittsburgh sunlight streamed through the window, casting a warm glow on his face as he carefully tore open the envelope that had arrived in the mail. His heart quickened with anticipation as he unfolded the invitation to his 25-year class reunion at Carnegie-Mellon University.

As Tom flipped through the pages of the invitation, memories flooded his mind like a tidal wave. He saw familiar names and faces, each one triggering a unique emotion. There was Sharon, their spirited stage manager who had always kept them on track during hectic productions. Brian, their talented lighting designer whose wit and sarcasm had never failed to make them laugh. And Andrea, their charismatic leading lady whose passion for theater had been both infectious and inspiring.

Excitement and apprehension swirled within Tom's chest. He wondered how his former friends had changed over the years, what stories they had to share. The thought of reconnecting with them filled him with a sense of joy and nostalgia. It was a chance to relive their college days, to reminisce about late-night rehearsals and unforgettable performances.

Closing his eyes for a moment, Tom allowed himself to be transported back in time. He remembered the thrill of stepping onto the stage, bathed in vibrant lights and eager applause. The camaraderie he had felt with his fellow actors and crew members was unparalleled—a bond forged through shared dreams and countless hours of hard work.

But life had taken them all on different paths after graduation. Careers, families, responsibilities—it seemed like only yesterday when they were young and full of boundless possibilities. Now, standing at the precipice of midlife struggles, the reunion offered an opportunity to reignite that spark, to rediscover each other and themselves.

With a determined smile on his face, Tom picked up his phone and dialed his friend and confidant from CMU, Jennifer Thompson's phone number. Her voice flowed through the line, filled with excitement and trepidation. They laughed and reminisced about their college days, catching up on the joys and challenges that life had thrown their way.

"I can't wait to see everyone again," Tom said, his voice brimming with enthusiasm. "To hear their stories, to share in their triumphs and struggles."

Jennifer's vibrant laughter echoed through the phone. "Yes, it'll be amazing to witness how we've all grown and evolved over the years. We were a family back then, and I believe we still are."

As they hung up the call, a renewed sense of connection settled over Tom. The reunion was not just a gathering of old friends; it was a celebration of their shared past and the possibilities that lay ahead. It was a chance to remind each other that their voices mattered—that despite the challenges of midlife, there was still magic within them waiting to be unleashed.

Tom leaned back in his chair and looked around his cluttered office, filled with memories and dreams. The theater scripts and photographs seemed to come alive, whispering stories of passion and resilience. There was a sense of purpose in the air—a feeling that this moment in time held so much promise.

With a spark of inspiration igniting within his soul, Tom started drafting an email to their former college friends. He carefully chose his words, infusing them with nostalgia and an invitation to embrace their own creativity once again. As he hit send, a surge of anticipation coursed through him.

The responses began flooding Tom's inbox—the familiar names and faces reaching out from across time and space. Each email brought forth memories, stories, and emotions long tucked away. With each reply, Tom felt the spirit of their college days rekindling within him—an exhilarating reminder of the dreams they had pursued together and the impact they had made upon each other's lives.

The road ahead may be uncertain, but Tom knew that the

reunion would be a turning point. It was a chance for dreams to be reignited, for connections to be deepened, and for the power of their collective imagination to once again shape their lives.

As Tom sat at his cluttered desk, surrounded by the remnants of their shared past, he couldn't help but feel a sense of gratitude. The reunion beckoned—a moment in time waiting to unfold. And with every email received, every memory shared, and every connection rekindled, Tom knew that they were all on the cusp of something extraordinary—a tale of rediscovery that would inspire them to embrace their own creativity and find new meaning in their lives.

2

Rekindling Connections: Tom and Jennifer arrive at the class reunion, reigniting old friendships after years apart.

In June 2021, Tom and Jennifer stood in line at the Carnegie-Mellon University 25 year reunion registration table, surrounded by a throng of excited alumni, eager with anticipation. The room buzzed with a symphony of laughter and chatter filling the air. It felt like a lifetime since they had last seen their former college friends, yet the memories remained vivid in their minds.

As they neared the front of the line, Tom's heart quickened with a mix of excitement and apprehension. He glanced at Emily Collins, whose eyes sparkled with anticipation. They exchanged nervous glances, silently acknowledging the shared emotions coursing through their veins.

Finally, it was their turn. Tom stepped forward, his hand shaking slightly as he reached for his name tag and program. The woman behind the table smiled warmly, sensing the significance of this moment for him. "Welcome back," she said, her voice filled with genuine warmth.

"Thank you," Tom replied, his voice tinged with gratitude. He glanced down at his name tag—it bore his name in elegant script, a tangible reminder of the person he had once been and the journey that had led him here.

Jennifer received her name tag next, her gaze fixed on it for a moment before she looked up at the woman behind the table. "It's good to be back," she said softly.

The room seemed to fade away as Tom and Jennifer moved to a quiet corner of the bustling registration area. Memories flooded their minds—the late nights spent rehearsing for theater productions, the moments of vulnerability shared with each other, the transformative power of creativity that had once bound them together.

Tom took a deep breath, savoring the familiar scent of anticipation that lingered in the air. "Do you remember our first play?" he asked Jennifer, his voice filled with nostalgia.

A smile tugged at the corners of Jennifer's lips as she nodded. "How could I forget? We were both so nervous, yet so determined to make it memorable."

They shared a knowing look, their eyes filled with the shared memories that had shaped their college experience. The late-night rehearsals, the adrenaline rush before stepping onto the stage, the laughter, and tears—they had weathered it all together.

As they moved through the crowd, Tom's eyes caught sight of Sarah Anderson, a former classmate with whom he had clashed during their time at Carnegie-Mellon University. Their unresolved conflicts had left behind a sense of tension that lingered beneath the surface.

Tom hesitated for a moment, then made his way towards Sarah. He approached her with a confident smile, hoping to bridge the divide that had once separated them. Sarah's gaze met his, and he could sense a mixture of surprise and uncertainty in her eyes.

"Sarah," Tom greeted her warmly, his voice filled with genuine warmth. "It's been a long time."

Sarah returned the smile, though there was a hint of awkwardness in her demeanor. "Tom," she replied, her voice laced with cautious optimism. "Good to see you."

They exchanged pleasantries, sidestepping the past as they navigated through memories that intertwined both pride and regret. The air crackled with unresolved tension, but underneath it all lay an unspoken understanding—a mutual desire to move beyond old wounds and forge a new connection.

Meanwhile, Jennifer's vibrant smile caught Emily Collin's eye from across the room. Jennifer rushed over, unable to contain her excitement at seeing an old friend after so many years. They embraced tightly, laughter mingling with tears as they relished in each other's presence once more.

Their conversation flowed effortlessly, as if no time had passed at all. They reminisced about their rebellious adventures and whispered secrets under starry skies. Jennifer's infectious energy brought a sense of nostalgia and a renewed sense of connection—reaffirming that the bond forged in their college years remained unbreakable.

At the CMU registration table, Tom and Jennifer had begun their reunion journey—immersing themselves in a sea of memories, reconnecting with old friends, such as Sarah and Emily, and savoring the magic of this present moment. The room hummed with anticipation, each interaction held the potential for new discoveries and unexpected connections. As with classmates, Michael Sullivan and David Grimly, who Tom, Jennifer, Sarah and Emily discovered later on; were reunited in conversation for the first time in 25 years.

As they navigated the reunion, Tom and Jennifer couldn't help but feel a spark of hope flicker within them. This reunion was not just about reminiscing—it was an invitation to embrace their own creativity once again, to find meaning in their lives and inspire one another. And as they made their way through the crowded room, they knew that this moment in time held limitless possibilities—a chance for dreams to be rekindled and profound connections to be forged once more.

3

Gone But Not Forgotten: Honoring Lucy's Memory

The Kresge Theatre fell silent as the group gathered for Lucy Shanahan's memorial, held by request of her family, in Carnegie-Mellon University's College of Fine Arts building. The group's footsteps echoed softly against the wooden floor. Each person carried a mixture of sorrow and gratitude for having known Lucy—a vibrant soul whose performances in this theater 25 years ago, left audiences breathless and whose presence left an indelible mark on those who knew her.

Sarah hesitated at the entrance, her heart heavy with loss. The walls of the Kresge Theatre were adorned with photographs capturing Lucy's infectious laughter and zest for life. It was as if each image held a piece of her spirit, frozen in time to be cherished forever. As Sarah took in the familiar faces surrounding her, she felt a bittersweet reminder of the joy Lucy had brought to their lives.

Tom followed behind Sarah, his eyes brimming with a silent

understanding. He greeted tearful friends with embraces, offering solace in shared sorrow. The weight of their loss lingered in every touch, every whispered conversation—a melancholy thread weaving through their collective grief.

Jennifer approached Lucy's family with trepidation, extending her condolences with gentle words and a touch that conveyed volumes of love and support. In their presence, Jennifer felt an overwhelming sense of strength—a testament to the support system that had surrounded Lucy throughout her life.

Emily and David stood at a distance, tears streaming down their cheeks. The sight of Lucy's family amplified the void that now existed—an absence that could never be filled. Yet, even amidst the ache of loss, Emily found solace in knowing that Lucy's spirit would forever live on in their memories.

As they gathered together, bound by the unbreakable threads of friendship woven through years of shared experiences, Tom reached out to gently place a hand on Emily's shoulder. His touch conveyed both empathy and strength—a silent reminder that they were not alone in their grief.

Embracing each other tightly in tearful hugs, the group sought comfort in shared remembrance—a collective act of honoring Lucy's life and the profound impact she had left on each of them. The room, filled with a sea of familiar faces, was burdened by the weight of their loss yet uplifted by the love they shared for Lucy.

Surrounding Lucy's family, a kaleidoscope of colorful flowers stood as silent witnesses to the love and grief that filled the room. Petals of vibrant hues served as a reminder that even in the face of tragedy, beauty and hope could still flourish.

Amidst the heaviness that weighed on their hearts, there was a palpable sense of gratitude—an acknowledgment that they had been blessed to have known Lucy. And as they gathered at her memorial, they found solace in the warmth of shared memories and the knowledge that her spirit would forever endure within them.

Together, they embarked on this journey of remembrance, holding tightly to the bond forged through years of laughter, tears, and shared experiences. In that moment, surrounded by photographs immortalizing Lucy's vibrant spirit, they drew strength from their collective grief—a testament to the power of friendship and the enduring legacy of a beloved friend.

As the Kresge Theatre remained hushed, the group took their places in a circle. Sarah's voice trembled slightly as she spoke, "Let us honor Lucy's memory by sharing our most cherished memories of her."

Tom nodded, his eyes filled with tears. He began, his voice filled with emotion as he recounted a moment when Lucy's contagious laughter had lifted everyone's spirits during a particularly difficult time.

Sarah followed suit, sharing how Lucy had selflessly helped her through a daunting audition, providing unwavering support and encouragement. Her voice wavered slightly as she conveyed the depth of her gratitude.

Michael reminisced about late nights spent with Lucy, fueling each other's creative fires as they dreamed of making their mark on the world. His infectious humor broke through the heaviness, bringing smiles to tear-stained faces.

Emily spoke softly, recalling Lucy's vulnerability and authenticity, which had inspired them all. Her voice cracked with emotion as she shared the profound impact Lucy had made on her own journey of self-discovery.

One by one, they shared their stories, laughter mingling with tears, creating an emotional tapestry woven with memories that spanned decades. In each word spoken, there was an unwavering love for Lucy—a determination to keep her spirit alive and carry her legacy forward.

As the room filled with heartfelt reminiscences, it transformed into a sanctuary of shared laughter and cherished moments. Through their stories, they celebrated Lucy's vibrant spirit, finding solace in the joy she had brought into their lives.

In the embrace of their collective grief, they discovered that even amidst the sorrow, love and friendship could be a guiding light. And as they continued to share their memories, the room seemed to fill with Lucy's presence once more—an ethereal reminder that although she may have left this world, her spirit would forever shine brightly in each of their hearts.

As they held hands and closed their eyes, their voices united in a song—a final tribute to their beloved friend. The melody, tinged with bittersweetness, soared through the room, its harmonies intertwining like threads weaving together a tapestry of shared memories.

In that moment, surrounded by the embrace of friendship and love, they knew that Lucy's spirit would forever be a part of them. And as the final notes of their song faded away, they found solace in knowing that her memory would live on in the hearts of those who loved her—a beacon of light to guide them through even the darkest of times.

4

The Birth of Dreams: Exploring the Formative Years at Carnegie-Mellon University

In the summer of 1991, Tom stood nervously in the dimly lit wing of the Kresge Theatre, surrounded by the soft murmurs of fellow aspiring actors. The air was thick with anticipation as they all awaited their turn for auditions. The scent of old wood and stage makeup wafted through the room, adding to the ambiance that filled every corner.

As Tom glanced around, he couldn't help but feel a surge of excitement mingled with a touch of apprehension. This was his moment to shine, to prove himself in the world of theater. He had spent countless hours practicing, perfecting his monologue, and now it was time to show what he was capable of.

The casting director called Tom's name, snapping him out of his thoughts and drawing all eyes towards him. With a deep breath, he stepped forward, his tall and well-built figure commanding attention even before he uttered a word. His charisma and determination radiated from him like an invisible force, garnering whispered admiration from his fellow auditionees.

Tom positioned himself center stage, the spotlight capturing his every movement. His dark hair fell slightly across his forehead, partially obscuring his piercing blue eyes that seemed to hold a world of emotions within them. With a swift nod to acknowledge the casting director, Tom took a moment to ground himself before launching into his monologue.

The words flowed effortlessly from his lips, each line delivered with conviction and raw emotion. He embraced the character he was portraying, allowing himself to become fully immersed in their world. Every word carried weight, resonating through the auditorium as if they held the power to transport the audience into another realm entirely.

As he reached the climax of his monologue, Tom's voice rose and fell with impeccable control. The sheer passion behind every word sent shivers down the spines of those watching. It was clear that Tom possessed a natural talent for acting, but it was more than just talent—it was a burning desire to bring characters to life, to touch the hearts of every person in that room.

When he finally finished, the Kresge Theatre fell into a momentary silence before erupting into applause. Tom's heart swelled with a mix of relief and pride as his peers acknowledged his talent. He had poured his heart and soul into this audition, and it was gratifying to see his hard work pay off.

As he left the stage, Tom couldn't help but feel a sense of fulfillment. This was what he was meant to do—to step onto a stage, embody different characters, and transport audiences into new worlds. The theater had always been his home, a place where he felt most alive.

With renewed confidence, Tom knew that his journey in the world of theater was just beginning. This audition was just one step on a path that would lead him to discover who he truly was as an actor. And as he walked out of the auditorium, he carried with him the knowledge that no matter what the future held, he had found his passion—a passion that would fuel his dreams and guide him towards his destiny.

Laughter and excitement filled the air as a young Michael Sullivan took the stage during a college comedy performance. The bright lights cast a spotlight on him, emphasizing his infectious smile and tousled brown hair. His eyes shimmered with mischief as he surveyed the eager audience that awaited his performance.

With a quick flick of his wrist, Michael adjusted the microphone stand to his preferred height. The crowd hushed in anticipation, their eyes fixed on him, eager to be entertained. Michael had always possessed an innate ability to bring joy to those around him, and tonight would be no exception.

As the first notes of upbeat music filled the Kresge Theatre, Michael began his routine with impeccable timing and quick wit. Each punchline was delivered with perfect comedic timing, eliciting roaring laughter from the audience. His ease on stage was palpable, as if he were simply chatting with friends at a local coffee shop rather than performing in front of a packed theater.

His jokes ranged from hilarious observations about everyday life to playful jabs at himself, ensuring that everyone could find something relatable in his routine. His natural charm oozed from every word he spoke, captivating even the most skeptical audience members.

Backstage, Emily Collins watched Michael's performance with a mixture of awe and admiration. She had always admired his ability to effortlessly bring levity to any situation. His humor was infectious, spreading like wildfire through the theater community and leaving smiles in its wake.

As the routine continued, Michael's boyish charm shone through, endearing him to everyone present. He interwove stories from his own life with absurd scenarios and exaggerated characters, effortlessly transitioning between each comedic bit. No topic was off-limits for Michael; he tackled everything from mundane daily tasks to societal quirks with both wit and sincerity.

The energy in the Kresge Theatre skyrocketed as laughter echoed off the walls. Michael's ability to find humor even in the darkest corners of life was a gift that had endeared him to his friends and classmates. It was in these moments, on the stage, that he truly flourished, bringing lightness and joy into their lives.

As his routine drew to a close, the crowd erupted into thunderous applause. Michael took a bow, his face flushed with a mixture of adrenaline and happiness. The gratification of making people laugh and temporarily lifting their burdens off their shoulders was an indescribable feeling—one that filled him with a sense of purpose and fulfillment.

As he exited the stage, Emily rushed to meet him backstage, her eyes sparkling with pride. "That was incredible, Michael!" she exclaimed, enveloping him in a tight hug. "You have a true gift for bringing laughter to the world."

Michael beamed, grateful for the support and encouragement from his dear friend. "Thank you, Em," he replied, his voice filled with genuine appreciation. "There's nothing quite like making people laugh—it's my way of making this world a little bit brighter."

Their embrace lingered for a moment longer before they broke apart, both knowing that the memories from tonight's performance would forever hold a special place in their hearts. It was through these shared experiences that their friendship had blossomed—a connection rooted in mutual understanding and an unwavering belief in each other's passions.

As they left the Kresge Theatre together, the echoes of laughter still reverberating in their minds, Emily couldn't help but feel inspired by Michael's ability to use humor as a force for good. His comedy had become a beacon of light in their lives—reminding them that even amidst the challenges they faced, there was always an opportunity for joy and laughter.

And as they walked side by side into the night, ready to take on whatever life had in store for them next, they carried with them the memories of this truly magical evening—a testament to the power of friendship and the transformative potential of laughter.

5

Rekindling Emotions

Tom's mind was still swirling with memories as he found himself lost in the past, overwhelmed by the weight of missed opportunities and unresolved feelings. It was as if time had become a fragile thread, connecting him to a world that no longer existed.

As he walked through the halls of their alma mater, Carnegie-Mellon University, flashes of laughter, rehearsals, and shared dreams flooded his mind. The theater season of 1995-1996 seemed like a lifetime ago, yet its impact on his life lingered, haunting him with what could have been.

He paused outside the familiar rehearsal room in the Margaret Morrison building, where he and Lucy had spent countless hours together, honing their craft and fueling each other's creativity. The door creaked open, inviting him inside, and he couldn't resist the pull of nostalgia.

The room was dimly lit, but the remnants of their presence still clung to the air. Tom stepped onto the worn wooden stage, feeling an electric current surge through him. This space had been their sanctuary—a place where they had explored different worlds through their performances, where their passions had intertwined.

His gaze swept across the empty seats, envisioning Lucy sitting there, her eyes burning with determination. A bittersweet smile tugged at his lips as he remembered her raw talent and unwavering commitment to her craft. They had pushed each other to new heights—testing boundaries and uncovering hidden depths within themselves.

Lost in his memories, Tom's thoughts drifted to one particular rehearsal. It was a pivotal moment in their relationship—when their connection began to transcend the stage. They were rehearsing a scene filled with intense emotions—love, longing, and aching vulnerability. As they performed together, their chemistry ignited into flames of passion that threatened to consume them both.

In that moment on the stage, Tom had caught a glimpse of what could be—a future defined by love and shared artistic endeavors. But fear and uncertainty had held them back, trapping their love in a realm of missed opportunities and regret.

The weight of those unspoken words settled heavily on Tom's shoulders as he stood alone on the stage. He wished for a chance to go back, to rewrite the script of their lives and seize the opportunity they had let slip away. But time was an unforgiving force—one that propelled them forward without regard for their longing hearts.

With a heavy sigh, Tom stepped off the stage and out of the rehearsal room, leaving Margaret Morrison and Carnegie-Mellon University behind a piece of his soul. The past would forever be a part of him, but he understood that he couldn't dwell in what could have been. It was time to confront the present, to embrace the reunion with open arms and an open heart.

As Tom walked back into the present-day world, he made a silent vow to seize every moment, to confront his unresolved feelings head-on. The journey ahead was uncertain, and the road might be littered with potholes of regret, but he knew that it was only by embracing the present that he could find peace and closure.

The theater season of 1995-1996 had shaped him in ways he couldn't fully comprehend. It had instilled in him a passion for storytelling, a hunger for connection, and an unwavering belief in the transformative power of art. And as he walked towards the reunion, he carried these lessons with him—ready to face whatever lay ahead and reclaim his voice in this ever-changing world.

Tom's footsteps echoed down the empty hallways as he embarked on this journey of rediscovery—a journey that would test his resolve, challenge his beliefs, and ultimately lead him to uncover the truth hidden within his own heart. And as he took each step forward, he knew that this reunion would not only reunite old friends but also rekindle dreams that had been dormant for far too long.

The stage had been his home once, a place where he had felt the most alive. Now, it was time to reclaim that home, to rediscover his passion, and to find the courage to embrace the future with an open heart. With each passing moment, Tom felt a flicker of hope ignite within him—a glimmer of possibility that reminded him it was never too late to pursue the desires that had been smoldering in his heart.

As he ventured into the unknown, Tom knew that his journey would be filled with unexpected twists and turns. But armed with memories of the past and a determination to uncover the truth, he stepped forward, ready to confront the unresolved love that had shaped him so deeply. The reunion awaited him with open arms—a chance for redemption, forgiveness, and the possibility of a love finally realized. And in this moment of rediscovery, Tom couldn't help but feel a renewed sense of purpose—a belief that dreams could be rekindled and destinies could be rewritten.

6

Navigating the Maze of Midlife

The room was filled with an air of anticipation as Emily stood before a group of eager faces. The sun streamed through the large bay windows, casting a warm glow on their expectant expressions. It was the perfect setting for Emily to share her journey—a journey that had taken her through financial struggles and forced her to confront her own fears and insecurities.

As she took a deep breath, Emily's eyes scanned the room, her gaze briefly meeting each person's gaze before settling on Jennifer Thompson, who sat interlacing her fingers with Tom. Their presence provided a comforting anchor—an unwavering support that gave her confidence to speak her truth.

"I've always prided myself on my independence," Emily began, her voice steady yet tinged with vulnerability. "But over the past few years, I've faced some significant financial challenges that have tested that independence to its core."

The room fell silent, the words hanging in the air like delicate threads waiting to be woven into a tapestry of shared understanding. Emily's words resonated deeply within each person—touching upon hidden fears and unspoken struggles that many had faced in their own lives.

She spoke of the pressures of climbing the corporate ladder—the demands of an industry that valued bottom lines over individual well-being. Her voice cracked slightly as she admitted the toll it had taken on her mental health, leaving scars that couldn't be seen but were felt nonetheless.

"But what hit me the hardest," Emily continued, her voice filled with determination, "was when I realized that my high-cost lifestyle had become unsustainable. I found myself suffocating under the weight of debt, drowning in a sea of material possessions that no longer held any true value."

The room seemed to hold its breath as Emily bared her soul—a raw honesty binding them all together. Each person could sense the weight of Emily's words—a mirror reflecting their own struggles with financial stability and the pursuit of an elusive sense of fulfillment.

Emily's gaze shifted to Tom, who nodded in understanding. His own experiences with financial uncertainty gave him a deep appreciation for the courage it took to confront those fears head-on.

"In my darkest moments," Emily confessed, her voice trembling slightly, "I feared that I would lose everything—my career, my home, my sense of self-worth. But it was through these struggles that I discovered a newfound resilience within myself—a strength born from necessity."

Jennifer squeezed Tom's hand, offering silent support as Emily continued her narrative. She spoke of the steps she had taken to reassess her priorities—to break free from societal expectations and define success on her own terms.

"I gradually started downsizing my life—letting go of material possessions that no longer brought me joy," Emily said, her voice growing stronger with each word. "I learned to appreciate the intangible riches in life—the relationships, experiences, and moments of true connection."

As Emily's story unfolded, the room became a sanctuary—a safe space for vulnerability and growth. Her journey resonated deeply within each person, reminding them of their own capacity for change and the power of redefining success.

"But perhaps the most important lesson I've learned," Emily concluded, her voice filled with hope, "is that financial struggles do not define our worth. Success is not measured solely by our bank accounts or material possessions—it is found in the richness of our relationships and the depth of our personal growth."

A collective sigh filled the room—a shared exhale of relief and recognition. Their eyes met, reflecting a newfound understanding of what truly mattered in life. The weight of financial struggles lifted ever so slightly, replaced by a renewed sense of purpose—a shift towards nurturing their personal well-being and embracing a more fulfilling path.

As they exited the room, the sunlight warmed their faces, casting long shadows along the corridor. Each person carried a piece of Emily's story within them—a reminder that financial struggles were not insurmountable obstacles, but rather opportunities for growth and self-discovery.

In their shared journey, they found solace and support—a reassurance that they were not alone in their challenges. And together, armed with newfound wisdom and resilience, they set out to embrace the present—to redefine success on their own terms and cultivate lives filled with authentic joy and fulfillment.

7

Lucy's Legacy: A Night of Reflection and Celebration

The room was abuzz with a quiet energy as the group of friends gathered in a beautifully decorated venue, adorned with pictures and memorabilia of their beloved classmate, Lucy. Soft lighting cast a warm glow on the photographs displayed on the walls, capturing moments frozen in time that reflected Lucy's vibrant spirit.

Tom, Sarah, Michael, Emily, David and Jennifer moved about the room, their steps careful and deliberate. They lit candles, their flickering flames symbolizing the everlasting light that Lucy still cast upon their lives. Each person took a moment to arrange flowers—a vibrant mix of red roses that mirrored Lucy's fiery personality.

As Tom hung a large portrait of Lucy on the wall, his hands trembled slightly with emotion. His fingers carefully adjusted its placement, ensuring that it captured her essence—the mischievous twinkle in her eyes and the infectious smile that had brightened their college days. He stepped back, taking in the sight before him, the weight of her absence palpable in the air.

Sarah moved gracefully around the room, her movements purposeful as she arranged clusters of candles. The soft glow illuminated Lucy's playful spirit, casting dancing shadows on nearby walls. With each candle she lit, Sarah felt a sense of connection—a flickering flame linking her heart to Lucy's eternal light.

Michael carefully arranged bouquets of roses, their petals velvety and rich in color. Their fragrance filled the air, mingling with memories and echoing Lucy's vibrancy. As he placed each rose in a vase, he couldn't help but imagine her standing beside him—an invisible presence reminding him of their shared laughter and adventures.

Emily carried an armful of programs and placed them meticulously on every seat. Her attention to detail ensured that everything was just right for this special evening—a testament to her love and admiration for Lucy. She stood back when she finished, taking in the sight of the room—a tapestry woven with memories and love.

The room was now transformed—an enchanting sanctuary where Lucy's spirit would be honored. As the group gathered in the center of the room, a hush fell over them. They looked around, their eyes drawn to the poignant decorations and the memories they held. A mixture of joy and sorrow filled their hearts, an exquisite blend of emotions that embodied their connection to Lucy.

Tom spoke first, his voice steady yet tinged with sadness. "Tonight, we come together to remember our dear friend Lucy," he began, his gaze flickering from face to face. "Her light may have left this world too soon, but it continues to shine brightly within each of us. Let us honor her spirit and celebrate the impact she had on our lives."

One by one, they stepped forward, sharing heartfelt stories that captured Lucy's essence—the moments that had shaped their friendship and left an indelible mark on their souls. Laughter mingled with tears as they reminisced about Lucy's infectious laughter, unwavering support, and passionate pursuit of her dreams.

Tom recounted a memory of Lucy's contagious laughter echoing through a rehearsal space—a moment that lifted their spirits and united them as a cast. Sarah shared how Lucy's unwavering support had carried her through a difficult time, reminding her of the beauty in the world. Michael regaled them with a hilarious mishap during a performance that had left them all doubled over with laughter—an unforgettable testament to Lucy's ability to find joy in even the most chaotic situations.

Emily spoke with admiration about Lucy's unparalleled talent for theater—a solo performance that had left the audience spellbound. Her words evoked the extraordinary range of emotions Lucy could convey, connecting her friends not only to her memory but to the transformative power of art.

As each story unfolded, a collective understanding grew—a tapestry woven from shared memories and unspoken connections. Their love for Lucy wrapped around them like a warm embrace, allowing them to find solace in the presence of their friends and the celebration of a life well-lived.

The room glowed with an ethereal beauty as the group reflected on the impact Lucy had on their lives. They felt her spirit intertwined with their own—a gentle reminder that even in her absence, she remained a powerful force that guided their paths.

As they stood together—Tom, Sarah, Michael, Emily, David and Jennifer—the room seemed to radiate with love and gratitude. In that moment, they knew that Lucy would always be with them, her memory forever etched in their hearts. And as they prepared to honor her further through music and prayer, they embraced the bittersweet beauty of remembrance—a testament to the enduring power of friendship and love.

8

The Theater's Call: Tom's Journey Back to the Stage

Tom stood at the edge of the Kresge Theatre stage, their rehearsal space for the performance. His heart racing with a mix of anticipation and nostalgia. The theater seemed to hold its breath, as if waiting for him to make his move. He took a deep breath, letting the familiar scent of the stage wash over him, grounding him in the present moment.

As he looked out at the empty seats before him, memories flooded back—performances that had left the audience spellbound, moments of vulnerability shared with fellow actors, and the exhilaration of bringing characters to life. This stage had been his home once, a place where he felt alive and connected to something greater than himself.

A soft smile tugged at the corners of Tom's lips as he recalled the countless hours spent rehearsing lines, perfecting movements, and finding the essence of each character. The dedication and discipline he had poured into his craft had shaped him in ways he couldn't fully comprehend until now.

Lost in his thoughts, Tom's attention was suddenly drawn to a door marked "Prop Room" at the side of the stage. Curiosity fueled his steps as he pushed open the heavy wooden door, revealing a treasure trove of forgotten relics from past productions.

The room was filled with props of all sizes and shapes—a dusty stack of books, worn-out furniture pieces, and even a weathered sword that had seen its fair share of battles on stage. Each item held a story, a connection to a performance that had left an indelible mark on Tom's soul.

He ran his fingers gently along the smooth surfaces of the props, remembering how they had become extensions of himself during those performances. They had been tools through which he explored different worlds, inhabited diverse characters, and touched the hearts of audiences.

In this room of forgotten treasures, Tom felt a renewed sense of purpose. It was as if these props were whispering to him, reminding him of the power of storytelling and the impact it could have on both the performer and the audience. The room seemed to come alive with the echoes of applause and laughter, fueling Tom's desire to create something meaningful.

Lost in his reverie, Tom was brought back to reality by the sound of footsteps approaching. He turned to find Professor Thompson, his former theater mentor, standing at the doorway. Her eyes sparkled with warmth and wisdom as she took in the scene before her.

"Tom," she greeted him with a gentle smile. "I had a feeling I would find you here."

"Professor Thompson," Tom replied, his voice filled with gratitude. "This place...it still holds so much magic."

The professor nodded knowingly and stepped further into the room, her gaze moving from prop to prop. "Yes, the magic of theater is timeless. It lives within these walls and within each of us who have been touched by it."

They stood in silence for a moment, their shared love for theater bridging the gap between past and present. Then, Professor Thompson turned to Tom, her eyes shining with encouragement.

"You have a gift, Tom," she said softly. "Your passion for theater is evident in every performance I've seen you give. Don't let it go to waste. The world needs your voice, your stories."

Tom's chest swelled with emotion as he absorbed her words. Here was someone who understood the depths of his yearning—the burning desire to create something extraordinary, to inspire others through the power of storytelling.

"I won't," Tom vowed, determination infused in his voice. "I will honor this gift and use it to its fullest potential."

Professor Thompson smiled warmly, her belief in him radiating from every pore. "I have no doubt that you will, Tom. Your journey is just beginning."

As they left the prop room behind and walked back onto the stage together, Tom knew deep in his heart that he had found his purpose. The stage was calling to him, urging him to create, to connect, and to make a difference. With each step he took, a newfound fire burned within him—a fire that would fuel his drive to create a successful theater company, one that would leave a lasting impact on both himself and the world.

And so, Tom set off on his journey, fueled by the love and support of his friends. With every step forward, he carried the memories of their shared experiences, the lessons learned from past triumphs and failures. The stage awaited him, whispering promises of untold stories and uncharted territories.

Tom knew that the road ahead would be challenging, but he also knew that he had rediscovered his purpose—the fire within him had been rekindled. And with his friends by his side, he was ready to embark on this new chapter of his life—a chapter filled with the magic of theater and the enduring power of friendship.

9

Past Shadows: Unearthing Conflict and Betrayal

The dimly lit room was filled with tension as Tom, Sarah, Michael, Emily, David and Jennifer gathered together. The weight of recent events hung heavily in the air, casting a shadow over their once-vibrant friendships. But they were determined to face the conflicts head-on and find a way to heal.

Tom took a deep breath, breaking the heavy silence that enveloped them. "We can't keep avoiding the elephant in the room," he said, his voice filled with determination. "We need to face these tensions and find a way to move forward."

Sarah nodded, her eyes shining with remorse and hope. "You're right, Tom. We can't change the past, but we can choose how we respond to it. We owe it to our friendship to find a path to forgiveness."

Michael's frustration seeped into his words as he spoke. "It won't be easy, but we've weathered storms before. We've been there for each other through thick and thin. We owe it to ourselves to try and repair the damage."

Emily's voice trembled with vulnerability as she added her thoughts. "It's going to take time and effort from all of us. We need to be honest with each other and truly listen. Only then can we begin to rebuild trust."

David's calm demeanor provided a sense of stability in the tense atmosphere. "Let's not forget why we became friends in the first place," he said. "We shared so many formative years together. That bond is worth fighting for."

As they delved deeper into their conversation, emotions poured out like rushing rivers that had been dammed for too long. Tears were shed, fears were expressed, and long-held grievances were aired.

But within that raw honesty, there were also glimpses of hope—small flickers of light in the darkness. Each person acknowledged their own flaws and mistakes, displaying a willingness to confront the demons that had driven them apart.

As the hours passed, the room transformed from a battleground to a sanctuary of healing. Through heartfelt conversations and heartfelt listens, they began to repair the damaged threads of their friendship. Laughter intermingled with tears as they reminisced about cherished memories and rediscovered the essence of their deep connection.

When they finally emerged from that room, there was a collective sense of relief and renewed purpose. They knew there was still work to be done, but they were ready to face it together. Their commitment to forgiveness and understanding resonated in their every word and action.

As they walked away, their footsteps echoed with resilience. They carried the weight of their past mistakes, but they also carried the seeds of redemption and growth. With each step forward, their bond grew stronger, forged anew through vulnerability and a shared desire for a better future.

And so, they embarked on their journey of healing—a journey filled with twists and turns, victories and setbacks. But they faced it as a united front, supporting one another through thick and thin.

As time passed, the scars of betrayal faded into faint lines on their hearts. Trust was rebuilt brick by brick, and their friendships bloomed once more. The resilience of their bond became a source of inspiration, reminding them that even in the face of darkness, love and forgiveness could prevail.

And so, they walked hand in hand into the unknown, ready to face whatever challenges lay ahead. For in the end, it was their commitment to one another that would guide them through—and in that commitment, they found solace and strength.

Their journey towards redemption was just beginning, but together, they were unstoppable. And with every step forward, they whispered words of forgiveness into the wind, allowing them to heal not only themselves but also each other.

In this moment, they understood the power of embracing vulnerability and choosing forgiveness. It was through these acts that they found their way back to one another, united in the shared understanding that their friendship was worth fighting for.

And as they continued on their journey, side by side, their hearts filled with hope and gratitude. For they knew that, no matter what lay ahead, their bond would endure—a testament to the enduring power of love and forgiveness.

10

Setting Differences Aside

Tom and Sarah sat across from each other in the cozy Pittsburgh coffee shop, their unease palpable in the air. The room felt small, suffocating almost, as they braced themselves for the difficult conversation ahead. The aroma of freshly brewed coffee enveloped them, providing a sense of comfort amidst the discomfort.

Tom took a deep breath, his voice filled with determination. "We can't keep avoiding the elephant in the room," he began, his eyes locked with Sarah's. "We need to face these tensions head-on if we ever hope to move forward."

Sarah nodded slowly, her gaze shifting towards her hands resting on the table. "You're right," she admitted softly. "It's been hard for me too, seeing our friendship strained like this." Her voice carried a hint of regret.

The weight of unspoken words began to lift as Tom leaned forward, his voice laced with vulnerability. "Sarah, I want you to know that our friendship means everything to me," he confessed earnestly. "We've shared so much together, and recent events have made me realize just how much I miss our connection."

Sarah raised her head, meeting Tom's gaze with a mixture of emotions flickering in her eyes. "I feel the same way," she whispered, her voice trembling slightly. "I've missed you too, Tom. It's been difficult without our bond."

Tears welled up in Tom's eyes as relief washed over him like a gentle wave. He knew they were taking the first step towards healing. "Sarah, it hurts me to see the distance that has grown between us," he admitted, his voice choked with emotion. "But we can't change the past. We can only learn from it. Our friendship is worth fighting for, don't you think?"

There was a flicker of hope in Sarah's eyes as she reached across the table and placed her hand on top of Tom's. The touch was tender, a symbol of their shared commitment to mend what had been broken. "Yes, it is," she agreed softly. "We've been through so much together, and I miss that deep connection we once had."

As they sat there, vulnerability began to bridge the gap that had formed between them. Walls crumbled, replaced by their shared desire for reconciliation. They slowly started to unravel the misunderstandings and unexpressed expectations that had fueled their conflicts.

Laughter mingled with tears as they reminisced about cherished memories from their college years—the late-night rehearsals, the impromptu adventures, and the endless conversations that fueled their dreams. Each memory served as a beacon of hope, reminding them of the strong foundation upon which their friendship was built.

The coffee shop became a sanctuary, a space for healing and understanding. Tom and Sarah found solace in each other's willingness to confront the past and strive for reconciliation. With every heartfelt word uttered, layers of hurt dissolved, replaced by an overwhelming sense of possibility.

By the time they left the coffee shop, a weight had been lifted from their shoulders. Their steps were lighter, their hearts fuller. The journey towards redemption had only just begun, but they were united in their commitment to heal their friendship.

As they ventured into the unknown, they carried with them the profound realization that true friendships are worth fighting for. Tom and Sarah were ready to face the challenges ahead, armed with vulnerability, understanding, and a shared desire for a deeper bond.

And so, hand in hand, they walked into the future—a future filled with renewed love, trust, and unwavering friendship.

11

Love's Uncharted Depths

Michael and Jennifer sat in a local Pittsburgh restaurant. The warm aroma of freshly fried pierogis enveloped them, creating a comforting atmosphere as they embarked on a conversation that would change the course of their lives.

Their eyes met, and in an instant, they both felt a connection that transcended words. It was as if they had known each other for years, their souls recognizing each other's presence. A flicker of hope began to dance in Michael's eyes as he realized that they shared similar desires and fears.

As they delved into heartfelt discussions, the walls they had built around their hearts began to crumble. They shared stories of heartbreak and disappointment with vulnerability and honesty, baring their souls to one another without judgment or pretense. In those moments, they found solace in each other's understanding and acceptance.

"I can't help but be drawn to your spirit," Michael confessed, his voice filled with genuine admiration. "The way you've overcome the challenges life has thrown at you is truly inspiring. It's rare to find someone who radiates such strength and resilience."

Jennifer blushed, her cheeks tinted a soft shade of pink. Her voice trembled slightly as she responded, "Thank you, Michael. I've had my fair share of struggles, but I've always believed in the power of perseverance. And meeting someone like you, who sees that in me, means more than you know."

Their conversation continued to flow effortlessly, with moments of laughter intermingled with moments of vulnerability. Time seemed to stand still as they sat there, immersed in their own world. The noise of the bustling coffee shop faded into the background, leaving only the sound of their shared laughter and whispered confessions.

"I never thought I would be in this place again," Jennifer admitted softly, her eyes glistening with unshed tears. "But meeting you has made me realize that it's okay to hope again, to believe in the possibility of finding lasting love."

Michael reached across the table, his hand coming to rest on top of Jennifer's. The touch sent shivers down their spines, filling them with a sense of warmth and comfort. "You give me hope too," he confessed earnestly. "I've been so afraid of getting hurt again, but being with you feels different. It feels like a chance to rewrite the story, to build something beautiful together."

As they sat there, completely present in each other's company, anticipation filled the air. Their hearts beat a little faster as they thought about what the future may hold. And as they walked away from that coffee shop, their steps were lighter, their souls rejuvenated by the possibility of a deep and meaningful connection.

The journey towards love and healing had just begun for Michael and Jennifer. They were no longer alone in their search for lasting happiness. Together, they stepped into the unknown, ready to embrace the challenges and joys that lay ahead. An unspoken understanding passed between them—a silent promise to be present for each other, to support one another through whatever may come.

In that moment, they began to understand the power of vulnerability and connection. Love may be uncertain and full of risks, but it was also the greatest adventure one could embark on. With open hearts and newfound hope, Michael and Jennifer started on this journey together, ready to embrace whatever the future held.

And as their intertwined fingers brushed against each other's, they knew that they had found something truly special—a love that had the potential to heal their wounded hearts and bring them closer to fulfillment than they had ever imagined.

12

Soul Searching

David found himself sitting in family's secluded, western Pennsylvania cabin, surrounded by the untouched beauty of nature. The walls of the cabin seemed to breathe with the calm rhythm of the forest, while rays of sunlight streamed through the window, casting a warm glow across the room. The stillness of the surroundings enveloped him, offering a respite from the chaos of everyday life.

As David ventured deeper into the wilderness, he found himself captivated by the power of symbolism in nature. He stumbled upon a babbling brook, its crystal-clear waters meandering through the rocks with purpose and grace. The sight drew him in, mirroring the ebb and flow of life's journey. It reminded him that just as the brook continued to flow despite obstacles in its path, he too had the strength to navigate the challenges that lay before him.

He sat on a fallen log near the brook, its cool surface grounding him in the present moment. As he observed the water flowing effortlessly over the smooth stones, he contemplated the significance of resilience and adaptability in his own life. He realized that like the brook, he had the ability to overcome obstacles and find his way forward.

Further along his trek, David came across a meadow adorned with colorful wildflowers. Butterflies danced among the blooms, their delicate wings carrying them effortlessly through the air. Each fluttering dance seemed to convey a sense of freedom and resilience. In this moment, David understood that life's challenges were not meant to be overcome with resistance but rather embraced and transformed into opportunities for growth.

In the meadow surrounded by vibrant wildflowers, David felt a surge of inspiration. He understood that life's beauty could be found in embracing its imperfections. Each petal represented a victory over adversity, reminding him that even the smallest victories were worth celebrating.

As dusk descended upon the cabin, David found himself standing beneath an awe-inspiring night sky filled with countless stars twinkling like distant jewels. The vastness of space stretched out before him, reminding him of his own insignificance in the grand scheme of things. And yet, he also felt a deep connection to the universe, realizing that he was a part of something much greater than himself.

Underneath the star-studded, western Pennsylvania sky, David marveled at the mysteries of the universe. He pondered the interconnectedness of all things, knowing that his journey was intricately woven into the fabric of existence. The silence of the night provided him with a sense of peace and serenity, allowing him to reflect on his place in the vast cosmic web.

As David sat there, enveloped by nature's embrace, he felt a deep sense of gratitude for these symbolic encounters. They had served as guideposts along his path, illuminating the way forward and helping him make sense of his own journey.

With each step back towards the cabin, David carried with him a renewed sense of purpose and clarity. Nature had provided him with a mirror through which he could understand his own struggles and triumphs. It had reminded him of the resilience and interconnectedness that lay within him.

As he settled down for the night, David knew that he was not alone in his search for meaning. The wilderness had become his companion, offering solace and wisdom in its silent presence. And with this newfound understanding, he drifted off into a peaceful sleep, confident in the knowledge that nature would continue to guide him on his journey of self-discovery.

13

Balancing Acts

As Emily stood outside Carnegie-Mellon's School of Drama's Purnell Center for the Arts, her heart pounding with anticipation. This was the first time in months that she had set aside time for herself, away from the demands of work and family. She took a deep breath, savoring the cool evening air, and pushed open the heavy doors.

As she entered the Purnell Center for the Arts, the ambient chatter and soft music enveloped her, creating an atmosphere of excitement. The walls were adorned with posters of past performances, each one promising an escape into a different world. A smile tugged at the corners of Emily's lips as she felt a sense of nostalgia wash over her. It had been years since she had immersed herself in the magic of live performance.

Emily found her seat, tucked away in the middle row. From here, she had a perfect view of center stage—the center of creativity and expression. The lights dimmed, casting a soft glow across the audience, and silence descended upon the theater.

The curtains parted, revealing a breathtaking set—a meticulously designed backdrop that transported the viewers to another realm. The actors stepped onto the stage, their presence commanding and captivating. Emily watched as they breathed life into their characters, their movements graceful and deliberate.

With each passing moment, Emily felt herself being transported into their world. She could feel the weight of their emotions—joy, heartache, longing—washing over her like a gentle wave. She laughed along with the humorous moments and felt tears prick her eyes during the poignant ones. The power of storytelling unfolded before her eyes, reminding her of the immense impact art could have on one's soul.

During intermission, Emily's mind buzzed with a renewed sense of wonder and inspiration. She joined the hum of conversation filling the lobby, eager to share her thoughts with other theatergoers. She struck up conversations with strangers, discussing their favorite moments and the themes that resonated with them.

It was during this intermission that Emily noticed an advertisement for a local dance class. A spark of curiosity ignited within her—a long-suppressed passion for movement seeking to break free. She made a mental note to look into it, realizing that reconnecting with her body through dance might be just what she needed.

The lights in the Purnell Center for the Arts dimmed once more, signaling the start of the second act. As the story unfolded,

Emily found herself fully immersed, hanging onto every word and gesture. The actors' performances touched something deep within her—an untapped well of emotion and creativity.

As the final scene played out, bringing the story to a close, Emily felt a sense of bittersweet joy wash over her. It was as if she had been on a journey alongside the characters, experiencing their triumphs and tribulations. The applause filled the theater, a testament to the impact the performance had on everyone present.

As Emily stepped out of the Purnell Center for the Arts, she carried with her a renewed sense of purpose and a burning desire to rediscover her own artistic passions. The theater had reminded her of the profound fulfillment she found in creative expression, and she knew that it was time to make space for it in her life once again.

With each step away from the theater, Emily felt a newfound energy coursing through her veins—a fire that had been reignited within her soul. She couldn't wait to explore the possibilities that lay ahead—whether it was through dance classes or revisiting her own writing and acting. The world was full of vibrant opportunities, waiting to be discovered.

Emily's journey towards self-discovery had only just begun, but she embraced it wholeheartedly. The theater had served as a catalyst for this newfound chapter in her life—a chapter where she would prioritize her own happiness and nurture her creative spirit. And as she walked into the night, guided by the flickering lights of the city, Emily knew that she was stepping into a future filled with limitless possibilities.

14

The Power of Teamwork

Tom's Pittsburgh apartment was abuzz with energy as Tom, Sarah, Michael, Emily, David and Jennifer gathered around a table covered in sketches, notes, and concept art. The room was filled with the aroma of freshly brewed coffee, invigorating their creative minds. They settled into comfortable chairs, ready to discuss their ideas for the upcoming theater production.

As they began to share their different perspectives and visions, the room became a springboard of possibilities. Tom's charismatic leadership shone through as he encouraged everyone to contribute their thoughts freely. The table quickly filled with scattered papers, each one representing a unique concept or theme.

The atmosphere was charged with excitement as they delved into passionate debates about the direction of the play. Charismatic and determined, Tom took on the role of mediator, carefully guiding the conversation while ensuring that each voice was heard. The room brimmed with creativity and potential as they explored ideas that pushed the boundaries of traditional theater.

The room was filled with tension as Sarah and Emily clashed over their differing perspectives. Each of them passionately defended their artistic choices, convinced that their vision was the right one for the theater production. Tom watched with growing concern, worried that this conflict could fracture their unity and derail the progress they had made.

"I just don't understand why you can't see my vision," Sarah exclaimed, frustration evident in her voice. "This play needs to be bold and daring, pushing the boundaries of traditional theater. We can't settle for mediocrity."

Emily crossed her arms and leaned back in her chair, a determined look in her eyes. "I appreciate your passion, but I believe subtlety and nuance can be just as impactful. We don't need to shock our audience; we need to engage them on a deeper level."

Tom knew that finding common ground was crucial. They needed to bridge the gap between these two opposing viewpoints to move forward. He interjected, breaking the tension in the room. "Both of your perspectives have merit," he said, his voice calm and steady. "What if we could find a way to incorporate elements from both visions? A balanced approach that challenges the audience while also allowing for introspection?"

Sarah sighed, her shoulders relaxing slightly. "I suppose compromise is necessary," she admitted, though a hint of reluctance remained in her voice.

Emily nodded, recognizing the need for middle ground. "You're right, Sarah. We shouldn't shy away from taking risks, but we also have to consider the emotional depth of the story. We want our audience to connect with the characters on a personal level."

Michael chimed in, his voice laced with wisdom and peace-making intentions. "I think it's important to remember that collaboration means listening to one another and valuing each person's input. There doesn't have to be a winner or a loser here; instead, we can create something greater than the sum of our individual ideas."

Tom nodded in agreement, grateful for Michael's words. He could sense the tension dissipating, replaced by a renewed sense of camaraderie. "Let's take a step back and reassess our goals," he suggested. "Perhaps we can find a way to merge Sarah's boldness with Emily's subtlety, creating an experience that challenges and engages the audience in equal measure."

As they revisited their sketches and notes, ideas began to flow once again. Sarah and Emily, now finding common ground, merged their concepts, blending vivid imagery with quiet moments of introspection. The room hummed with excitement as they explored new possibilities, bringing their once-divergent visions together.

Over the next few hours, compromises were made, egos set aside, and the play began to take shape. It was a delicate dance of collaboration, each member contributing their strengths while embracing the ideas of others. Through respectful dialogue and open-mindedness, they found a balance that honored both risk-taking and emotional resonance.

By the end of the rehearsal, the group had crafted a cohesive narrative that seamlessly wove together elements from each individual's vision. As they stepped back to admire their work, a shared sense of pride washed over them. In that moment, they knew they had achieved something special—a production that embodied the power of collaboration and compromise.

Tom couldn't help but smile at the sight before him. "We did it. We found a way to showcase all our strengths while creating something truly unique."

Sarah leaned back in her chair, a satisfied grin spreading across her face. "I have to admit, this is far better than anything I could have come up with on my own."

Emily exchanged a knowing glance with Michael, her eyes shining with newfound respect. "It just goes to show the magic that can happen when we embrace different perspectives and work together."

David raised his cup of coffee in a toast. "To collaboration and compromise—the keys to unlocking our creative potential."

As they clinked their cups together, a sense of unity engulfed the room. They knew that their journey was far from over, but they were filled with a renewed sense of purpose and confidence. Together, they would bring their collective vision to life, showcasing the power of collaboration and compromise for all to see. And as they continued on this artistic journey, they were certain that their theater production would be a testament to the strength of their friendship and shared artistic passion.

15

What Could Have Been

Tom sat alone in his study, surrounded by faded photographs and dusty theater memorabilia. The room was dimly lit, accentuating the melancholic atmosphere. Rays of sunlight streamed through the partially closed blinds, casting slivers of light onto the worn wooden desk. A sense of nostalgia hung in the air as Tom's eyes wandered to a framed picture on the wall, capturing a moment from their college years.

His gaze fixated on the photograph, his fingers tracing the edges lovingly. The image depicted him and Lucy, arms wrapped around each other, their smiles wide and carefree. Tall bookshelves lined the walls, filled with weathered scripts and dog-eared novels, bearing witness to countless rehearsals and shared laughter. Tom couldn't help but wonder what could have been if he had taken a chance on love all those years ago.

A heavy sigh escaped Tom's lips as he leaned back in his leather armchair, lost in a sea of regrets. Charismatic and determined, his normally confident demeanor seemed momentarily subdued.

Thoughts swirled in his mind, replaying moments spent with Lucy and imagining an alternate reality where he mustered the courage to pursue a relationship. He contemplated the joys and struggles they could have shared, wondering if he made the right choice in holding back.

The sound of a slamming door downstairs jolted Tom out of his reverie. His heart raced as he recognized Sarah's familiar footsteps ascending the staircase. She had always been perceptive and had a knack for picking up on his moods.

"Tom? Are you up here?" Sarah called out, her voice tinged with concern.

Tom quickly composed himself, wiping away any trace of vulnerability from his face. "I'm here, Sarah," he replied, his voice steady.

Sarah entered the study, her vibrant energy filling the room. Her eyes flickered with curiosity as she glanced at the photograph that had captured Tom's attention. "What's on your mind, Tom?" she asked, her voice gentle yet probing.

Tom hesitated for a moment, unsure of how much to reveal. But he trusted Sarah, knew she was a loyal friend who would listen without judgment. "I've been reflecting on the past," he admitted, his voice tinged with regret. "Specifically, my relationship with Lucy."

Sarah took a seat opposite Tom, her gaze filled with empathy. "It's natural to wonder 'what if,'" she said softly. "But we can't change the past, Tom. All we can do is learn from it and make the most of the present."

Tom nodded, his eyes wandering back to the photograph. "I know, but sometimes it's hard not to dwell on the missed opportunities," he confessed. "Lucy was special, and I often wonder if I made the right choice in not fully pursuing a relationship with her."

Sarah reached out and placed a comforting hand on Tom's arm. "Regret is a heavy burden," she said gently. "But remember, we were young and uncertain back then. We didn't fully understand ourselves or what we wanted. It's okay to have regrets, but it's also important to forgive yourself and focus on the future."

Tom let out a deep breath, feeling a weight lift off his shoulders. Sarah's words resonated with him, reminding him that dwelling on the past would only hold him back. The present was where he could make amends and embrace new possibilities.

"You're right, Sarah," Tom said, a glimmer of determination shining in his eyes. "It's time to let go of regrets and focus on what lies ahead. We have an opportunity to create something beautiful together, something that honors our past while embracing the present."

Sarah smiled warmly at Tom, her eyes sparkling with excitement. "You're absolutely right, Tom," she agreed. "Let's seize this moment and make the most of it. Our shared creativity and friendship have the power to create something truly magical."

As they sat there, enveloped in the comforting embrace of their friendship, Tom felt a renewed sense of purpose and possibility. The past could not be changed, but the present was theirs to mold. And together, with their collective vision and unwavering determination, they would bring their dreams to life once again.

16

Letting Go of Perfection: Sarah's Journey to Embrace Imperfections

Sarah sat at rehearsal with the group, distracted. Sarah felt the weight of her thoughts about unfinished tasks pressing down on her. Sarah remembered the papers piled up around her desk, back at the office; a chaotic mess that mirrored the whirlwind her life was in. Tom and Emily worked quietly together, only amplifying the mounting pressure Sarah felt.

Minutes turned into hours as Sarah tried to keep up with her self-imposed high standards. Each task seemed more daunting than the last, and the weight of perfectionism bore down upon her shoulders. Her face tightened with tension, lines etching deeper with each passing moment. The relentless pursuit of flawlessness consumed her thoughts and stirred anxiety within her.

As deadlines loomed closer, Sarah found herself trapped in a never-ending cycle of self-doubt and fear of failure. She meticulously examined each task, searching for any imperfection that threatened to undermine her meticulous work. Every decision felt paralyzing, every choice laden with consequences.

But as the pressure reached its peak, so did Sarah's breaking point. A surge of intense stress and anxiety washed over her, threatening to engulf her completely. Her hands trembled as she gripped the edge of her script, desperately seeking stability amidst the chaos. Tears welled up in her eyes, unshed emotions bubbling to the surface.

In that moment, Tom, Michael, Emily, David and Jennifer noticed Sarah's distress. Concern filled their expressions as they gathered around her on stage, their presence a comforting balm to Sarah's troubled soul. Their eyes radiated empathy, their unwavering support shining through.

"Sarah, you don't have to face everything alone," Tom said gently, placing a hand on her shoulder. "We're here for you."

Michael nodded in agreement, his voice filled with reassurance. "You've always been there for us when we needed it. It's only fair that we return the favor."

Emily's warm smile echoed their sentiments. "You're not failing by asking for help," she said softly. "It's a testament to our friendship and shared goals."

Sarah felt a glimmer of hope stir within her, a spark that could ignite the pathway out of her self-imposed struggles. Gratitude washed over her as she realized she didn't have to bear the weight alone. She had a support system, a group of friends ready to navigate the challenges together.

Taking a deep breath, Sarah mustered the courage to voice her concerns. "I'm overwhelmed," she admitted, tears glistening in her eyes. "I've been striving for perfection, but it's suffocating me."

Tom's eyes filled with understanding as he squeezed her shoulder gently. "You don't have to be perfect, Sarah. None of us are. We're here to share the load and help you through this."

David nodded fervently. "You've always had our backs. Now, let us have yours."

Emily reached out, taking Sarah's trembling hand in her own. "We'll rise together, Sarah. You don't have to bear this burden alone."

In that moment, Sarah felt a flicker of relief. The weight on her shoulders began to ease as she embraced the collective strength of their friendship. She realized that asking for assistance wasn't weakness—it was an acknowledgment of their shared journey and the belief that they were stronger together.

Tears streamed down Sarah's cheeks, mingling with the raw vulnerability exposed in that moment. And as her friends enveloped her in a supportive embrace, she knew she wasn't alone anymore. Together, they would navigate the challenges ahead and overcome the obstacles in their path.

Sarah took solace in knowing that even in the face of uncertainty and imperfection, their friendship would serve as an anchor—a guiding light through the storm. With their unwavering support, she could confront her fears and find healing in the arms of those who cared for her.

In that tender moment of shared understanding, Sarah glimpsed the power of vulnerability and the strength that came from admitting her struggles. As her friends surrounded her, love and empathy filled the room, erasing the suffocating grip of perfectionism that had held her captive.

From that day forward, Sarah vowed to embrace imperfections as opportunities for growth. She would learn to delegate tasks and trust in the capabilities of her friends. No longer burdened by the need for flawlessness, she would forge a new path—one paved with shared responsibilities, mutual support, and the liberating joy of true collaboration.

17

Breaking Free: Confronting Fear and Embracing Connection

At work, Michael gently squeezed the white, Styrofoam coffee cup as he poured the freshly brewed pot. As Michael smelled the fresh aroma of coffee pouring, the weight of the upcoming confrontation with his difficult colleague, Alex, beared down on him. The tension in the office was palpable, each passing moment only intensifying the unease between them.

As the time for their meeting grew closer, Michael could feel his heart pounding in his chest. He had rehearsed the conversation in his mind countless times, trying to anticipate every possible response from Alex. But now, as reality set in, he couldn't help but feel a surge of nervousness.

Taking a deep breath, Michael returned the coffee pot on the maker, turned back around and made his way towards Alex's workspace. Every step felt heavy, as if he was carrying the weight of the entire office on his shoulders.

The atmosphere around them seemed to grow even more tense, as if the room held its breath in anticipation. Finally, Michael reached Alex's desk and cleared his throat, mustering the courage to speak. "Alex," he began, his voice steady despite the tremor in his hands. "Can we talk for a moment?"

Alex looked up from his computer, an air of indifference radiating from him. "What do you want?" he replied curtly. Michael took a deep breath, reminding himself to stay calm and focused. "I wanted to discuss our interactions during team meetings," he said firmly.

"The constant criticism and dismissiveness towards my ideas are affecting our ability to work together effectively." Alex scoffed, leaning back in his chair. "Your ideas aren't worth anything anyway," he retorted dismissively.

Michael felt a surge of frustration welling up within him, but he pushed it aside. This was not the time to get caught up in emotions. He needed to remain composed and level-headed.

"I understand that we may not always agree on everything," Michael said calmly, trying to maintain eye contact with Alex. "But it's important that we respect each other's opinions and find a way to collaborate more effectively." Alex rolled his eyes, a smug smile playing on his lips. "Why should I listen to you? Your ideas are always flawed."

Michael took a deep breath, refusing to let Alex's dismissive comments get to him. He had prepared for this moment, and he knew that staying calm was key. "This conversation isn't about the quality of my ideas," Michael replied firmly. "It's about creating a positive and supportive work environment where everyone feels valued and heard."

For a moment, silence hung in the air, their gazes locked in a battle of wills. Michael could see the flicker of doubt in Alex's eyes, as if his facade of indifference was starting to crumble. Finally, Alex spoke, his voice softer than before. "I didn't realize how much my behavior was affecting you," he admitted reluctantly. "I guess I've let my own insecurities get the best of me." Michael nodded, his voice filled with understanding. "We all have our struggles," he said sincerely. "But it's important that we find ways to support each other and create a healthier work environment."

A sense of relief washed over Michael as he realized that his words were resonating with Alex. Perhaps there was hope for change after all. "I'm willing to make an effort," Alex finally said, a hint of vulnerability in his voice. "Let's find a way to move forward and improve our working relationship."

Michael smiled, a genuine warmth spreading through him. This was the outcome he had hoped for—a resolution born out of open communication and understanding. "I appreciate your willingness to work things out," Michael replied gratefully. "Together, I believe we can create a more harmonious and productive work environment." As they parted ways, Michael couldn't help but feel a sense of accomplishment. By facing his fear of confrontation head-on, he had not only addressed the issue with his difficult colleague but also paved the way for deeper connections and a more positive work dynamic.

Walking back to his desk, Michael felt a newfound sense of confidence and empowerment. He knew that he had taken control of his own narrative, and in doing so, he had opened doors to personal and professional growth. From that moment forward, Michael vowed to embrace confrontation as an opportunity for growth and understanding.

He understood that it wasn't something to be feared, but rather a chance to foster stronger relationships and create positive change. As he settled back into his seat, ready to tackle the tasks ahead, Michael couldn't help but feel a sense of pride. He had faced his fear head-on and come out stronger on the other side.

And with this new outlook, he was ready to face any challenges that lay ahead, knowing that he had the power to navigate them with grace and resilience.

18

Unraveling Perfection: David's Journey to Embrace Imperfections

David sat alone in a cozy, Pittsburgh coffee shop, his mind consumed with thoughts of past relationships gone wrong. The weight of these failed connections bore down on him, casting a shadow over his present happiness. He traced the rim of his coffee cup with his finger, lost in a sea of memories and regrets. As he sat lost in thought, a sudden collision jolted him back to reality.

Papers and books scattered across the floor, mingling with those of a stranger. David looked up to see a woman standing before him, her eyes wide with surprise. A smile slowly spread across her face, radiating warmth. "Oops! I'm so sorry," she said with a chuckle, crouching down to gather the fallen papers. David's lips curled into a small smile as he joined her in collecting the scattered items. There was something about this unexpected encounter that brought a glimmer of light to his cloudy thoughts. As they straightened up and returned to their seats, David found himself engaging in conversation with this woman named Maya.

Their voices filled the air with animated enthusiasm as they compared book recommendations and shared snippets of their lives. It was as if the universe had orchestrated this serendipitous meeting, knowing that David needed a fresh perspective. Maya spoke of her own journey in embracing imperfections, how she had learned to find beauty in life's uncertainties and unexpected detours. Her words resonated deeply with David, as if they were the balm his soul had been yearning for all along. The hours slipped away unnoticed by both David and Maya as they delved deeper into their discussion. The coffee shop buzzed around them, unaware of the profound connection blossoming between two strangers.

With each word spoken, David felt a weight lifting from his shoulders. Maya's wisdom seeped into his consciousness, softening the edges of his overanalytical mind. She taught him that not everything had to be perfect, that sometimes imperfections brought forth the greatest lessons and growth. As the sun began to set outside, casting a warm glow through the coffee shop windows, David realized that he was no longer lost in the past. Through Maya's guidance and their meaningful conversation, he had found a way to release the burdens he had carried for far too long. And in that small corner of the coffee shop, surrounded by the aromas of freshly brewed coffee and the gentle hum of conversation, David made a choice. He would embrace imperfections, let go of the need for absolute certainty, and allow life to unfold with its twists and turns.

As he bid farewell to Maya, gratitude filled his heart. He knew that this chance encounter had been a turning point in his journey towards self-acceptance and personal growth. And as he stepped back out into the world, ready to face whatever uncertainties lay ahead, he carried with him the wisdom of imperfection and a newfound sense of peace. The coffee shop faded into the background as David walked away, his mind no longer burdened by past failures. He saw the world with new eyes, noticing the beauty in every imperfection. Life still held its mysteries, but now he was ready to embrace them. With each step forward, David felt a lightness in his spirit and excitement for what lay ahead. He didn't know where this newfound perspective would lead him, but he trusted that it would guide him towards greater fulfillment and personal growth.

And as he embarked on this new chapter of his life, David couldn't help but feel a renewed sense of hope and possibility. The uncertainties no longer overwhelmed him—they inspired him to step outside his comfort zone and embrace the imperfect journey that awaited him. In that moment, David understood that life's imperfections were not obstacles to overcome, but rather opportunities for growth and transformation. And as he walked into the sunset, he carried with him the wisdom and warmth of Maya's words, forever grateful for the serendipitous encounter that had changed his life.

19

A Night of Reckoning

The Purnell Center for the Arts at Carnegie-Mellon University was alive with anticipation exactly one month after the night of the 25 year reunion for the class of 1996; as the night of the performance finally arrived, in July 2021. Elegant decorations adorned the space, evoking a sense of nostalgia and transporting the attendees back to their college days. Glittering chandeliers cast a warm glow over the polished wood floor, illuminating the sparkling dresses and sharply tailored suits. The room hummed with excitement, filled with the joyous chatter of old friends reconnecting after years apart.

At the center of it all stood Tom, exuding his trademark charm and enthusiasm as he greeted each guest with genuine delight. His charismatic presence seemed to fill the room, drawing people towards him like moths to a flame. He radiated joy as he caught up with Jennifer. Their conversation was punctuated by laughter and shared memories, underscoring the deep connection they had maintained over the years. Sarah quickly joined them.

Meanwhile, Michael worked the room effortlessly, his affable nature putting everyone at ease. He engaged in lighthearted banter with old friends and acquaintances, reminding them of the importance of cherishing their friendships. His easygoing demeanor brought smiles to faces that hadn't seen genuine happiness in far too long. Emily and David found themselves near the dance floor, their eyes sparkling with anticipation as they observed their friends reconnecting.

Just a few steps away from the lively dance floor, a table covered in photo albums and scrapbooks became a hub of conversation and nostalgia. The characters huddled around it, flipping through pages filled with faded photographs and handwritten notes. Each image captured a moment frozen in time – late-night rehearsals, backstage shenanigans, and unforgettable performances that still held a special place in their hearts.

As they reminisced over the old photos, their faces lit up with laughter and recognition. Tom paused at a picture of him and Lucy, his gaze lingering on her radiant smile. A mixture of fondness and melancholy washed over him as he recalled their complicated past. The group shared stories about their shared aspirations, the struggles they faced, and how they supported each other through triumphs and failures.

With each turn of a page, their memories wove together like an intricate tapestry, reminding them of the moments that had shaped their lives. Sarah shared anecdotes about their late-night study sessions, their laughter filling the air with warmth. The characters found solace in these shared memories, cherishing the bonds they had formed during their college years.

But the night in Pittsburgh was not just about reminiscing; it was also about celebrating and letting loose. The DJ started playing a familiar tune, its infectious rhythm pulsating through the ballroom. Without hesitation, the characters made their way to the dance floor, their feet tapping to the music as they let go of any inhibitions. Laughter echoed throughout the room as they swayed to the beat, forgetting their worries for a moment and embracing the freedom that came from being surrounded by loved ones.

Tom took center stage to start the performance, inviting his classmates up to join him for a group dance. The characters obliged, and soon the dance floor became a vibrant sea of joyful movement. Their bodies moved in sync, their spirits soaring with elation as they celebrated this rare gathering. Jennifer's infectious energy ignited the dance floor as she led the group in spontaneous choreography. Michael's quick wit kept everyone entertained, while Emily and David found themselves locked in a spirited dance battle. The dance floor became a microcosm of their journey – a testament to their resilience and collective spirit.

Amidst the revelry center stage, Sarah and Emily sought solace in each other's company, finding a quiet corner towards the side of the stage, away from the vibrant festivities. They sat down, their faces reflecting vulnerability and determination. Driven by shared experiences, they opened up about their insecurities, fears, and dreams. Sarah spoke of her struggles with the pressure to succeed, while Emily listened intently, offering a warm-hearted and compassionate presence.

In this moment of vulnerability, Sarah and Emily realized the strength that came from embracing their true selves. They made a pact to prioritize their own well-being and chase their dreams fearlessly. Fueled by renewed determination, they returned to the festivities, ready to face the challenges that lay ahead.

The characters formed a circle in the center of the Purnell Center stage, their faces reflecting a range of emotions – anticipation, nervousness, and hope. Tom took a deep breath, his charismatic presence commanding attention as he spoke from the heart. He expressed his regret over past misunderstandings and acknowledged the pain they had caused one another.

One by one, the characters shared their own heartfelt apologies and sought forgiveness for past mistakes. Tears flowed freely as they acknowledged the wounds that needed healing, recognizing the growth they had experienced individually. The circle became a space of empathy and understanding, fostering an environment of love and acceptance.

As forgiveness was exchanged, a sense of renewal filled the air. The characters embraced each other tightly, acknowledging the power of second chances and new beginnings. Their shared journey had brought them full circle, from unresolved love to rediscovery, from personal struggles to collective healing. With hearts lighter and spirits rejuvenated, they looked towards the future with hope and anticipation.

The night of the reunion had brought back together 6 former classmates for the first time in 25 years. That night of the reunion would merely be a turning point towards the night of their return performance, in collaboration with Carnegie-Mellon University. That night, that moment in time, had become a milestone in their lives – an evening filled with closure, forgiveness, and new beginnings.

As the Purnell Center for the Arts continued to pulsate with energy and laughter, the classmates reveled in the knowledge that they were not alone on their respective journeys. They always had and would always have each other.

20

The Power of Artistic Awakening

Tom, Sarah, Michael, Emily, David and Jennifer found themselves standing on the threshold of their new creative retreat – David's family cabin, nestled in the midst of towering trees and tranquil surroundings. The air tingled with excitement as they stepped inside, feeling the weight of anticipation settle upon their shoulders.

The western Pennsylvania cabin exuded warmth and charm, its cozy interior providing the perfect sanctuary for their artistic exploration. The characters dispersed, each finding their own space to settle in and embrace the solitude that awaited them.

As days turned into nights, the classmates engaged in exercises designed to tap into their creativity. Sarah found solace in the expansive windows that overlooked a serene lake. With a paintbrush in hand and colors at her disposal, she gave life to vibrant landscapes that captured the essence of her dreams.

Michael retreated to the porch, where the rustle of leaves and gentle breeze served as his muse. Armed with pen and paper, he poured his humorous observations onto the page, weaving tales that evoked laughter and reminded people of the joy found in simple moments.

Emily immersed herself in the basement-turned-studio, surrounded by canvases, brushes, and tubes of paint. With each stroke, she explored new techniques and pushed boundaries, creating abstract masterpieces that defied traditional norms.

Sarah went into the kitchen and got lost in the aromas and textures of preparing and cooking food for everyone as she rehearsed a new audition monologue.

David sought solace in the library, losing himself in well-worn books and ancient wisdom. He allowed himself to sink into philosophical contemplation, unraveling ideas and concepts that would infuse the production with profound depth and resonance.

Jennifer got away from everyone, hiking and discovering trails and her character voices.

Tom took refuge in the attic-turned-rehearsal space, where he meticulously crafted scenes that reflected their personal journeys. His vision came alive through improvised performances, transforming mere words on paper into transcendent moments that tugged at heartstrings.

In between their solitary pursuits, the classmates would gather around a crackling fireplace, exchanging stories and insights.

They marveled at each other's progress, realizing how much growth had occurred during their time together.

With each passing day, their creativity blossomed and interwove, each character's unique strengths and perspectives complementing the others. The lines between reality and art blurred, as they embraced vulnerability and allowed their experiences to inform and shape their performances.

Late into the night, Sarah, Jennifer and Emily found themselves engrossed in a deep conversation by the flickering firelight. They spoke of their fears and insecurities, unearthing the vulnerabilities that had long been hidden away. They encouraged each other to step out of the shadows and reclaim their true selves, supporting one another in their pursuit of creative fulfillment.

Meanwhile, Michael and David engaged in their own spirited debates, challenging each other's perspectives and pushing the boundaries of their understanding. Their intellectual sparring ignited new ideas and transformed mere thoughts into powerful insights that would resonate with audiences.

As the days dwindled down, the characters reconvened in their designated spaces for one final creative push. They poured their souls into each brushstroke, word, and movement, fully embracing the transformative power of their collective creativity.

Finally, the time came to share their creations with one another. In a final gathering around the fireplace, they bared their souls through impromptu performances, tears streaming down their faces as they witnessed the raw beauty of their collective talent.

With hearts full and spirits alight, the classmates knew that they had accomplished something extraordinary - they had breathed life into their dreams and created a production that transcended their individual aspirations. They reveled in the opportunity to perform again together at Alma mater, Carnegie-Mellon University, one more time.

David's family cabin, now stood as a testament to the power of creativity - a sacred space where the classmates and artists had rediscovered themselves and forged bonds that would endure beyond this moment in time. Although there were no solid plans scheduled for another reunion, the classmates and friends promised to keep in touch.

As the classmates bid farewell to the west Pennsylvania cabin, its walls infused with their laughter, tears, and artistic energy, the classmates carried within them a renewed sense of purpose and an unwavering commitment to follow their creative callings. They understood that their voices mattered, that their unique contributions were needed in a world hungry for inspiration and genuine connection.

Together, they embarked on the next chapter of their midlife journey – ready to face the challenges that awaited them, armed with the transformative power of creativity and an unbreakable bond forged in the crucible of their dreams.

About the Author

Tate was born Timothy Sean, in Saint Petersburg, FL. in 1974, living there with one older sister and a loving family. Tim enjoyed youth baseball and football into high school at Gibbs, graduating from the Pinellas County Center for the Arts (PCCA) and moving to Pittsburgh in 1992, to attend the acting conservatory at Carnegie-Mellon University. At PCCA and CMU, Tim was trained under world renowned faculty in the theatre arts. Research, development and creation of a character; leading into show specific performance choices, scene work, Blackbox theatrical performances and finally, large auditorium sized venues filled with hundreds or thousands of audience members, all packed in together, their energy palpable on stage the moment you enter. Tim spent the summer of 1994 living in the United Kingdom, First, residing in London's Piccadilly Circus district. Then, Tim moved up to Balliol College in Oxford, studying Shakespeare and classical writing. Later, Tim met his father, who had travelled over from the US, and the two travelled the southern half of Ireland together, the McGhees home country. The McGhees spent a significant portion of the week on the western coast. This included a stay in Galway and an overnight trip on Inishmaan (one of the Aran Islands) where Tim hiked with his dad to find one of his favorite writers, John Millington Syne's chair, to pray.

Back in America, Tim went on to act in leading and character roles in mainstage and network productions for PCCA, Carnegie-Mellon University and after graduation with honors in May of 1996, after a brief residency in the West Greenwich Village neighborhood of New York City, Tim moved to Los Angeles in the fall of 1996, after signing with the Cosden Talent Agency in Hollywood. In 1997, Tim guest starred on NBC's Saved by the Bell, CW's Sweet Valley High, and then received the SAG guest starring role, on USA's Pacific Blue, where Tim took the SAG union name, Tate, Living off the Sunset Strip in West Hollywood, working in film, commercials and television for 6 years, Tate continued creating and writing his own poetry and short stories, as part of the artistic training he had received from his earlier days attending PCCA "Exhibit X." and CMU. Tate entered and performed his one man show "The Savage Window,' written in college, for the National Poetry Conference held in Anaheim, CA. in 1999. Tate continued acting under the new direction of a personal manager, also writing two feature screenplays: HOPE and SILVERGIRL, during that time; until the fall of 2001, when Tate was offered an opportunity to return to graduate school and work towards a master's degree in applied behavior analysis from the Florida Insititute of Technology (FIT.)

Back in Florida in 2002, Tate committed to the new career in Behavior Analysis, working with those in need back in St. Petersburg, FL. In 2010, Tate and his wife got married on the beach. Tate and his wife welcomed their first child, a son, in 2012. In 2014, Tate welcomed the birth of their new daughter. Meanwhile in 2014, Tate was also invited to Bosnia and Herzegovina to present of a special assignment as a Behavior Analyst. Tate took residence in Paris for the month of November of 2017, writing from the Saint Michel neighborhood, witnessing the beauty of the Notre Dame cathedral only months before the destructive inferno. In 2019, Tate continued writing, leading to the episodic series THIS MOMENT IN TIME, now available on Kindle Vella and later the feature screenplay GANGPLANK. In 2023, Tate is currently practicing ABA now over 20 years and continuing to develop several other projects. Tate enjoys service, spending time with his family, writing, movies and music, following/attending sports games, concerts, surfing, Today, Tate thanks Jesus Christ above all else and looks to be a loving husband, father, friend to all, practicing BCBA and author with participation across many genres. THANK YOU FOR YOUR INTEREST.

Also by Tate McGhee

Legends of Paradise Key

In a coastal Florida neighborhood on the brink of destruction from rampant development and rising sea levels, a group of close-knit friends embark on a thrilling adventure to unravel a century-old legend. They must navigate treacherous swamps and crumbling mansions as they outsmart greedy developers and ancient curses in their quest to find a lost diamond necklace rumored to possess mystical powers. This gripping tale combines environmental activism with magical realism, offering a fresh perspective on the fight to preserve home and heritage. With its richly developed characters and immersive setting, this suspenseful journey will captivate readers who crave mystery, intrigue, and themes of friendship and the power of legends.

King of the Night

A young boy named Miles discovers courage, knowledge & bravery in the dark of the night after he meets a cat named Shadow. Together they travel a mythical journey far and wide overcoming fear while unlocking the beauty of imagination.

www.ingramcontent.com/pod-product-compliance
Lightning Source LLC
Chambersburg PA
CBHW070642130626
46555CB00006B/2665